THE
SHARP
EMPIRE

TYLER JOHNS

Order this book online at www.trafford.com
or email orders@trafford.com

Most Trafford titles are also available at major online book retailers.

Printed in the United States of America.

ISBN: 978-1-4669-8804-0 (sc)
ISBN: 978-1-4669-8805-7 (e)

Trafford rev. 03/28/2013

 www.trafford.com

North America & international
toll-free: 1 888 232 4444 (USA & Canada)
phone: 250 383 6864 ♦ fax: 812 355 4082

Dear Readers: As you read this book there are strange creatures like revived dinosaurs, mammalian reptiles (therapsids), talking intelligent animals and more.

CONTENTS

INTRODUCTION

I now introduce a cobra named, Hieronymus Sharp. He once gained many amounts of quantum education of everything in the universe. He can be described as a scientist, historian, scholar, philosopher, sorcerer and much more.

One day, a secret phantasmal force gave him the legs of a lizard and he was humanized into a scary reptilian beast. He made himself gray-colored clothing and a long black robe to put over it (with wide sleeves like a wizard's robe). Then he put on a brown leathery vest. If you could see, his actual height is about seven feet and one inch tall with a neck measured about one foot and a half. He also wears thick plastic black boots with clear plastic at the toe parts, showing his toes. He crowned himself as an emperor, with a crown in the shape of a rounded cross.

He had also decided to run an empire of monstrous creatures, using his sorcering powers to revive certain extinct species of prehistoric grudge. The soldiers and officers were crocodiles, raptors (with short hooked beaks or long, straight beaks), thick-skinned, bipedal, dinosaur-like lizards; and gorilla-like, tyrannosauric beasts called, monáchis (which have tiny, needle-sharp claws that stick on any material of a wall like an insect or a spider). There are also officers as cassowaries, normal lizards, or half-mammal half-reptile creatures.

They had a celestial white condor named, Artidector who had powers to revive dead animals and people. He was also a great teacher of courage from fear until he was banished from the Death Scale (the Sharp Empire's home biosphere) by the emperor, for his mistakes talking about the good that will conquer his evil.

Sometime later, the emperor needed an advisor to take his place. He sent his soldiers, known as pirate knights, who were fierce, strong fighters wearing cobalt suits of armor and helmets. They also had iron or steel straps and belts that held chest plates that fended off their enemies' blaster shots, made out of the same metal as the straps. The straps ran both vertical and horizontal (which ran under their arms). On top of their helmets were the rounded crosses, which symbolized their empire.

They were immortal (all soldiers and officers, including the emperor), all including the monsters on the Death Scale. If they had gotten wounds or bruises, there could be thousands of tiny robots, rather than blood cells in the human circulatory system, fighting and destroying any bacteria with one zap and the ability to repair the wounds or bruises in a flash, creating thick metal scabs, which cannot come loose until their skins were repaired. Also, their hearts were replaced with plastic, vacuum-like pumps with rubber valves that can pump the blood even faster than a normal animal's heart. They were impervious to high blood pressure, heat, drought, suffocation, and many other risks.

Anyway, many of the pirate knights were sent to Earth to find a grave, to dig a human corpse (on any grave that would say a good message about a family). Well, they found a fat one that would fit into a large, bulky crab-like robot that the emperor had built. Back on one of their ships, a scale cruiser, they set the corpse in the hind half of the body on an operating table. Then they put on the front half with a front belly cabinet, six crustacean legs, four-foot long arms with seven-fingered hands, and three mechanical brains. For the face, they gave him two large eyes, one for the left brain and one for the right brain. Then for the top middle brain they gave the robot three mechanical eyes that sought time. The right eye told the past and can record messages with holograms, the middle eye told the present and has an ability to look further by zooming, and the left eye told the future and has the ability to hypnotize. The real eyes can move in different directions without running out of focus. Soon, the robot was complete. He was given the name, Darth Waternoose. The table sprung up and the emperor used his revival powers to bring the robot to life. The eyes lit up and a loud breathing noise was happening, blowing through the slits of the mouthpiece. Waternoose broke the wrist clips of the table then walked forward by the docking bay of the scale cruiser and roared out loud. He gained education on the empire. He was also given a light saber.

Yes, also this empire has powerful electrical/energetic weapons such as light sabers, laser axes, bomb-erangs (boomerangs that blow up when thrown), noble gas-colored energy-secreting zorchers, shockwave clubs, etc. They can use them to defeat their enemies quickly.

Their enemy was a force of earthly animals of faith, humanized to stand on their hind limbs and bearing intelligence, called the Heaven Federation. The soldiers and pilots were mainly canines, felines, and bears. Both males and females work for this force. For both of these teams, they combine armed forces like the army and the navy (sometimes air force or marine corps) in one force called a mega force. As for the Sharp Empire, they are all males. Here are the proper adjectives for each side: Sharp Empire=Serpential, Heaven Federation=Heavenly Federal.

As to think about space safety, they would always have to wear warm clothing (at least dogs, cats, and bears have fur to keep themselves warm). Also to keep the temperature normal, they could use a cold fluid in tubes or containers under their armor. In need for food, they might not eat for a while or so. They would just eat beef, poultry, fruit, vegetables, and anything depending on the animals' species. As for thirst, they would just carry containers of water in the breast pockets of their suits, using a long extendable tube to suck in the water. For excretory emergencies, males wear a foamy pair of trunks with a long tube where their genitals fit in a cup-like funnel part which lets urine flow through the tube into a container wrapped around one leg while the females wear an extra-absorbent diaper under their trousers. This should catch the fact of how we, modern humans, use a toilet. (Also the Heavenly Federal pilots or soldiers have holes in the seat of their trousers for their tails.) For fecal emergencies, they use a bag to cover the rear for the releasing of feces. Well in their home stations or bases they have co-restrooms (in which male and female use at the same moment, but at least they have doors for private stalls). All things there for space toilets; and columns that fill with water for bathing: the soldiers and pilots use a breathing machine for oxygen while they're in the water-filled bath columns. (Mask, tube, and air vent)

Now, since I just finished the methods of safety uses and needs, (also for health emergencies, they might provide medicines and first aid bandages) you'll just find the ideas and get them. You'll see if the bad guys win or if a hero or group of heroes helps the Heaven Federation, and so on.

THE SERPENTIAL ORIGINS

From an unknown constellation, a small system of planets had been foreign and strange to those who don't know it. The star died years later and then a new system was created. The evil emperor, Hieronymus Sharp used his sorcery powers to turn this once thriving system into nothing. He was also successful in exiling many fantasies that were created by humans for their children's interests, using his creational biosphere, the Death Scale.

Several years later, the Heaven Federation noticed strange activity coming from the Death Scale. A team of heroes was hired, a lioness named, Nala Boomer (whose parents had died from an unknown disease caused by a monster), a wasp named Zinger Warsp (who gives advice whenever he appears) and Skinamarinky-Dinky-Dink Skinamarinky-Doo (which was a classic children's song until an orangutan was given this name, probably by the soul of such an imaginary character) were sent to investigate.

Upon their arrival, they met the celestial white condor, Artidector, who gave Boomer the chances of this most challenging quest and the purpose of recovering hope and peace. Boomer was trained by a clever dragon named, Dermazzo Joustiáño (dehr-MAHT'so hoos'tee-AHN'yo), who trained her in welfare and combat. But by a matter of unwelcome to the Death Scale, Joustiáño betrayed his apprentice and joined the Sharp Empire as a count. Nala Boomer, Zinger and Skinamar were captured by the empire's armored lizard soldiers called, scale troopers. They threw them in prison as Boomer was being held up for execution. Skinamar and Zinger barely escaped the Death Scale and returned home to tell the Heaven Federation about their friend's fate. The Sharp Empire used a large machine called the "Spruce Noose". They decided to hang Boomer, her paws bound with a pair of brass binders and a gag in her mouth, so that she wouldn't call out for anyone to save her. A rubber hangman cord was lowered from the Spruce Noose. Boomer's neck was wrapped in the loop then an officer pulled a lever to higher the cord. Then there was the tragic death of Nala Boomer.

A few years had passed, Emperor Sharp had again intended to eliminate other fantasies, and ordered his henchmonsters to guard his biosphere. The Heaven Federation must turn to a new team of heroes to have Artidector take care of them. A team must be strong enough and wise enough to tell the truth of the Sharp Empire and free the galaxy once again.

CHAPTER 1

FORCES OF FAILURES

It is a futuristic period of war. Heavenly Federal
spies have stolen the plans to the Sharp Empire's ultimate
weapon, the Death Scale, an inhabited armored biosphere
with enough power to destroy an entire world of fantasies
from stories, children's television, etc.
The betrayed Irish princess, Mariana Izodorro was
commanded to hide the plans from the enemy, so that the
Heaven Federation can restore freedom to the galaxy. But
at these battles and intensions, they always failed . . .

It was surely a bad idea to steal the Sharp Empire's plans. A
scale cruiser was chasing the princess's starship, firing laser
cannons back and forth. The scale cruiser's shield reflected
the royal starship's cannon shots while the royal starship's
shield ran out of power and the engine slowed down. The

scale cruiser moved over the royal starship then opened the under hatch, where the ship was pulled in. Heavenly Federal soldiers readied their firearms in the entrance way. All of a sudden, a spark line was cutting open the door then it exploded. An army of scale troopers appeared. All fighters shot back and forth, at this the Heavenly Federal soldiers were dead, because they could not stand a chance, neither male nor female. The scale troopers made way for the robotic lord, Darth Waternoose, walking his crab-like legs over the soldier corpses, and breathing loudly all the time. He looked around then flicked his finger to have the troopers follow him. What was hiding was the princess with Skinamar and a human-like robot called the "Invisi-Bot". The princess had to send a message to Earth. She gave it to Skinamar and the Invisi-Bot and those two escaped into a hole that had an escape pod. Then they fell to Earth.

Meanwhile, Waternoose lifted up a male canine soldier by the neck. He heard a communication saying: The plans are hidden in the main deck. If no sign of them exists, all passengers must be attempted to be arrested.

Waternoose choked the soldier in his hand saying, "Where are those transmitters? *What* have you done with those plans?"

"Well, uh . . ." the soldier could not resist suffocation, ". . . I . . . I gave 'em to . . . someone in . . . there . . ." He tried to point where he put the plans, but it was his time to die. He fell to the ground. Waternoose put up an uproar.

"Come on, men; tear this ship apart," he said, "until you find those plans. And bring me its passengers, I want them alive!"

The scale troopers obeyed. They searched everywhere until they found the human female with long blonde hair, which was the princess. She tried firing at them and to escape, but a trooper shot a stunning ray at her. She fell, lying on the floor. The troopers bound her hands with brass binders as they lifted her up to stand. They marched with her to Waternoose, waiting by the entrance.

"Darth Waternoose," the princess was confronted, "you've sufficiently murdered and assassinated those who believed in the dreams of my family."

"I have been confirmed to sophisticate your philosophy and wonders in this holocaust of yours, your highness," said Waternoose. "I want to know what happened to the plans they sent you."

"I don't know what you're talking about," said the princess. "I'm a member of the Serpential Senate . . ."

"You are part of the Heavenly Federal alliance and the traitor to the cause," Waternoose darted back. "Take her away!" The scale troopers obeyed him.

The Serpential commander, Karbono Kassow (a cassowary) walked toward Waternoose to tell the truth.

"The monitor was lying," he said. "The plans are nowhere to be found."

"If your father knows the truth," said Waternoose, "the princess is the only one to tell us where the enemy base is."

"She'll die before she'll tell us anything."

"Leave that to me."

The Serpential governor, Kalvino Kassow (the father of the commander) came by as Waternoose was walking with the commander, now standing.

"Lord Waternoose," the governor called.

"Yes, Governor Kassow," said Waternoose.

"We need to fix the monitor so we'll find the plans easier," said the governor.

"Your son may have the answers."

The governor went ahead to check on his son as Waternoose thought about what made the monitor lie.

CHAPTER 2

HELP SEARCH

And so, on the planet Earth, Skinamarinky-Dinky-Dink Skinamarinky-Doo and the Invisi-Bot landed in Ireland on a grassy field with hills of clovers. Is this the luck of the Irish? Perhaps there never is or was.

"This place is unbelievable," said the Invisi-Bot.

"It looks like a predicament to me," said Skinamar, pulling the grass. "Besides we need a new master or mistress."

"Yeah, well there are none to be found here," said the Invisi-Bot. "I'm going this way. You can go your way while I go mine."

"Hey, wait a sec," Skinamar spotted a giant vehicle. "I spy a transport."

"Have you lost your mind, Skinamar?" asked the Invisi-Bot.

"No, but I just see leprechauns leaping towards us."

Skinamar was right. A horde of leprechauns was coming for them. The two fellows ran for cover, but a leprechaun launched his giant net toward them. There was no escape for Skinamar and the Invisi-Bot. The leprechauns carried them into their giant van-like vehicle. Then they drove them to an old village in the middle of the island.

CHAPTER 3

IRISH FARM

So, the leprechauns took many things they had found throughout Ireland to an old farm nearby. Here we should find one of the heroes for later in the story: Martino Izodorro, the elder brother of Mariana Izodorro, whose parents were assassinated by the emperor. Martino had to live with his aunt and uncle on this old farm (as it sort of looks like a countdown to the Dark Ages). He couldn't even be a prince in any matter of rule for his family.

The leprechauns showed up with their giant vehicle, running a flea market with animals, robots, old machine parts, and other things. They all cost gold coins to give the leprechauns their pot luck. They even sang riddles about the items they have.

Anyway, Martino's uncle, Rowan, was about to buy some of those major items. A leprechaun was showing the Invisi-Bot, saying, "This strange mechanical thing turns invisible, How very inconceivable. That would be twenty gold pieces."

"Sure, I'll take that, thank you," said Rowan, paying for the robot.

Martino just looked at some amazing things the leprechauns had. The Invisi-Bot came up to him and said, pointing at Skinamar, still hanging on a bar, "Excuse me, sir, but that orangutan is in need for you, I believe."

"Uncle Rowan!" Martino called out.

"Yeah," his uncle said back.

"What about that ape thing?" Martino asked.

"How much is the orangutan? My nephew's wondering," said Rowan.

"Fifteen pieces," said a leprechaun.

"Here's a big piece worth twenty," Rowan gave the leprechauns a large coin.

"Ooh, what a way to pay," said one of the leprechauns, quite amazed, "here's your change. Have a good day." He flicked five coins to Rowan.

Just some moments later in the house, Skinamar decided to take a bath. The Invisi-Bot needed some oil and cleaning. At least Martino knew how to manage the two travelers. The Invisi-Bot was very intelligent, working with expensive appliances that are futuristic. He and Skinamar watched television for two hours.

"Don't you guys ever get tired of watching T.V.?" Martino asked, as he walked in the lounge.

"Well at least it's just reality happening on it," said the Invisi-Bot.

Skinamar was walking down the hall with a towel around him.

"Well, since you can *talk,*" said Martino, "why don't you guys introduce yourselves?"

"Well alright," said the Invisi-Bot, reminded. "I am the Invisi-Bot, a robot built by creatures from above, or wherever. And this is my loyal companion, Skinamarinky-Dinky-Dink Skinamarinky-Doo."

"Hello," said Martino.

"Howdy," said Skinamar. "Just call me Skinamar."

"I've been on many adventures through space," the Invisi-Bot began the story. "Of course I had to fix a ship. I use this switch . . ." he showed the switch he was talking about on his waist. ". . . to turn invisible when there is any emergency maneuvering. You should be lucky that this war is not on this planet of yours . . . ."

"You know the Heaven Federation against the Sharp Empire?" Martino wondered.

"Indeed we do," the Invisi-Bot continued his story, "we once had two other companions named Zinger Warsp and Nala Boomer."

"Really," Martino was amazed, "what were they like?"

"Nala Boomer was a lioness," said the Invisi-Bot. "She was a well-being animal heroine until she was condemned as an intruder and hanged. Zinger Warsp, our good friend the wasp, was a good advisor to us along with sidekick, Skinamar. And now I got this other thing to tell you . . ." He handed Martino a disk-shaped object that looked like the face of a watch. ". . . we were on this starship captured by a scale cruiser, one of the ships built by the Sharp Empire. We were with this girl, who was a human like you. Would you like to see for yourself?" He pointed to the face-like object as Martino turned the knob on the side.

Suddenly, as he turned it until it could work, a hologram appeared from the pit of the object, saying, "Please, please, I must have a rescuer." It was, of course, Princess Mariana Izodorro.

"Haven't I seen such a face in years?" Martino wondered. The message was repeating.

"That girl is a princess," said the Invisi-Bot. "She is by the name of Mariana Izodorro."

"Mariana?" Martino had a thought. "Oh my word, that sounds like my sister. I remember all that when I was just a kid; before my parents died."

"Well, you have such an infinite term memory," said the Invisi-Bot.

"Uh, guys," Skinamar interrupted, "I think if you turn the knob all the way back to its starting position, it will just play the entire message."

"Good idea," Martino agreed. He turned the knob the opposite direction of where he turned it. Then a click at all the way back turned it off. "Oops," he said, "okay, I'll just figure it out some other time." He gave the recorder to Skinamar. Then he stood up.

"Guess that was your lucky charm of the day," said Skinamar.

"Marty!" Martino's aunt, Mara, called through the hallway. "I've just fixed some dinner. My husband and I are waiting."

"Okay, I'll be right there, Aunt Mara!" Martino called back. "I'll see you guys after dinner," he said to Skinamar and the Invisi-Bot. So as Martino went to the kitchen, the other two spent the evening watching the giant screen television.

CHAPTER 4

STRANGE FEELINGS

While Martino, his aunt, and his uncle were having potato soup with gravy for dinner, Martino had a strange thought about his sister being captured.

"Those guys told me these amazing stories about this war in space," said Martino. "They said they had two other friends missing. I wonder if they were even real." He ate a scoop of his soup. His mind was scrambling, causing him to start a conversation with his aunt and uncle. He continued, "They said their names were Zinger Warsp and Nala Boomer. Then they said that Zinger character was a wasp and a good advisor. And this Nala Boomer lioness was executed by this empire called the 'Sharp Empire'."

"Well," said his uncle. "I don't think that lioness was real. She's just a legend and so is that wasp." He gobbled another scoop of his soup.

"Oh," said Martino. "I guess they were wrong." He felt traumatized about the way Skinamar and the Invisi-Bot told those stories. "They also said that I had a sister . . ."

"Yeah," his uncle interrupted, "she was kidnapped after your parents' death."

"They knew my parents?" Martino was satisfied.

"That's a long story. Tomorrow, I want you to organize the robot and orangutan, so they are ready for the convention in Athlone."

"Okay, I'll keep an eye on them."

Later in the evening, after dinner, Martino followed his uncle's instruction about Skinamar and the Invisi-Bot. Suddenly, the Invisi-Bot was still in the house but Skinamar disappeared by that sudden moment.

"Hello," said the Invisi-Bot, appearing behind the couch in the lounge. Martino was distracted.

"Where's Skinamar?" he asked.

"Perhaps he's out looking for help again," said the Invisi-Bot.

"Oh great," said Martino. He dashed into the closet and found his uncle's binoculars. Then he and the Invisi-Bot dashed out the front door.

Martino used the binoculars around the outside farm. He and the Invisi-Bot stood next to each other as Martino turned the knob to zoom the binocular vision.

"He should be out in the fields loafing about," said the Invisi-Bot.

"He's nowhere in sight," said Martino lowering the binoculars. "D*** it!"

"Ah ah, watch your mouth," the Invisi-Bot snapped.

"Sorry," said Martino.

"Martino!" his uncle called out. "I'm turning the power off!"

"Alright, I'll be there in a minute!" Martino called back. "See you later, I gotta go," he said to the Invisi-Bot. He dashed back to the house as the Invisi-Bot stood by the farm, waiting for him in the morning.

CHAPTER 5

THINGS GET STRANGER

The morning arrived. Rowan was walking around the house searching for his nephew.

"Martino!" he called out. "Marty! MARTY!" He walked back in the house then found his wife in the kitchen, frying bacon and boiling lettuce.

"Have you seen Martino this morning?" he asked her.

"He said he had something to do before today, so he left early," Mara answered.

"Did he take that robot and orangutan with him?" asked Rowan.

"I think so," said Mara.

"I'll see if I can get a hold of him," said Rowan. He went by the TV to get the phone.

Meanwhile, Martino and the Invisi-Bot were out to find Skinamar in Martino's uncle's old, old pick-up truck.

Suddenly, the radio communicator machine beeped. Martino answered it.

"Martino," it was his uncle. "Where are you?"

Martino answered, "I lost the orangutan and I'm out looking for him."

"Well then be home on time," said his uncle. "I don't want to be late for the convention."

"Will do," said Martino. His uncle hung up.

Martino and the Invisi-Bot arrived among the clover fields, and then found Skinamar between two giant rocks.

"Skinamar!" Martino called out.

"Marty?!" Skinamar heard the call. He was standing between the giant rocks. Martino and the Invisi-Bot parked the truck and jumped out, then headed for Skinamar's location.

"Skinamar, we don't have time for this," said Martino.

"We'll have no more stories to tell anyone," said the Invisi-Bot.

"Well, I was trying to find some others to get us off this planet," said Skinamar.

"Well, we don't have time," said Martino, "there's a convention my uncle has to catch."

Just as they headed back to the truck, a horde of leprechauns was surrounding it. Martino took out his uncle's binoculars to see what they were doing.

"I see those leprechauns, taking the truck apart," he said. "Wait," he saw a leprechaun move, "there's one leprechaun ahead, now he's gone."

"Hello!" a leprechaun appeared in front of him. Martino screamed and jumped in shock.

"Sorry," said the leprechaun, "I wondered what you were doing."

"It doesn't concern you," said Martino.

"Well," said the leprechaun. "I was just . . ." PAK! ". . . A-oh!" Skinamar stretched his arm and punched the leprechaun away.

"Emergency maneuvers!" shouted another leprechaun. "Orangutan fighter awaits us!" All of the leprechauns leaped toward the three adventurers. One had a sling shot that flung a rock at Martino's forehead. He fell lying to the ground. Others jumped after Skinamar. He spun on his head to smack the leprechauns using his arms as top blades. The Invisi-Bot was in cover under a rock.

All of a sudden, a buzzing sound occurred around the air, towards the rocks. It scared the leprechauns as it filled their pointed ears.

"Find some cover!" a leprechaun shouted. Many of the others hid between the rocky dens.

"Somebody save me!" another leprechaun shouted. "I'm allergic to bees." Another leprechaun called him. Then he went to where that other leprechaun showed him.

Skinamar ducked and covered his eyes as Martino lay on the ground.

CHAPTER 6

MEET ZINGER WARSP

The sound came from an old giant wasp. This might be the wasp, the Invisi-Bot was telling Martino about. The wasp hovered over Martino, still lying on the ground from a leprechaun's sling shot. Skinamar appeared from his hiding place.

"Zinger?" he noticed the wasp.

"Well howdy," said the wasp. "Come here, my ape friend, there's nothing to be afraid of." Skinamar went towards him.

"Master Zinger Warsp?" the Invisi-Bot came out of his hiding place. "Long time no see."

"What sort of mess has your human friend gotten into?" asked Zinger.

Martino awoke when he heard the talking.

"Zinger?" he said. "Z . . . Zinger Warsp? Boy, am I glad to see *you* in real life."

"Tell me, young man," said Zinger, astonished. "What brings you out here in the wilderness?"

"This orangutan," Martino said, pointing to Skinamar. "He's been trying to get us off this planet. This invisible robot and he were telling me stories about this war in space. They talked about you, and they said that you guys had a lioness friend named, Nala Boomer. Was *she* really a friend of yours? Do you know what they're talking about?"

Zinger had a thought. "Nala Boomer," he said. "Nala Boomer . . . . Now that's a name I haven't heard in a long time; a long time."

"I think my uncle's heard of her," said Martino. "He said she was just a legend."

"Oh, she wasn't a legend," said Zinger. "Not quite."

"Do you know her, though?"

"Of course, I know her," Zinger was barely growling. "You thought right; she *was* a friend of mine."

"Well, I guess you guys are reunited."

Zinger lowered himself down towards Martino and asked, "What is your name? I haven't asked."

"Martino Izodorro," Martino said, getting up off the ground.

Zinger led him, Skinamar and the Invisi-Bot to his home dome high in the sky. He had to carry them with his legs as they held on to one another's ankles. When they got to that dome, Zinger introduced the three travelers his home and said, "Welcome to my basic home, just make yourselves comfortable." The three travelers sat on the rocky furniture.

"Now, I should say," Zinger said, "I've got gifts for you." He hovered to a high shelf with old white boxes. He grabbed them within his six jointed legs, and then he lowered down to the stick-built table within the furniture. He showed a box to Martino, reaching his front legs toward the edge of the lid. In the box were two firearm-like devices. Martino grabbed them out.

"What are these?" he asked.

"They are electronic digital disk launchers," Zinger told him. "Some of the weapons built from a fantasy by my friend, Artidector. I once gave them to your father when he fought in a war of combat until his assassination. He wanted you to have these when you were old enough, but your uncle wouldn't allow them."

Martino gave one shot through the round window on the side of the dome.

"Whoa! Watch yourself out there," Zinger warned him.

Suddenly, Martino had a memory scramble, "Oh speaking of . . . I'm supposed to go with my aunt and uncle to this convention with Skinamar and the Invisi-Bot today. If I'm not home by that time, I'm in huge trouble."

"Save your breath," Zinger calmed him down. "There's nothing to worry about. I still have a couple things for your friends." He gave the other two boxes to Skinamar and the Invisi-Bot.

Skinamar opened the box in front of him and found a periscope-like firearm. He was amazed and satisfied.

"That is the sun ray phaser," Zinger told him. "Its fuel is absorption of the sun's energy. It can be used to melt down complex planetary materials and elements."

Then the Invisi-Bot looked in the last box. He found a shiny black cube with solid tubes on some of its faces.

"What could this be?" he asked.

"It's an upgrade for your invisibility," said Zinger, zooming toward the Invisi-Bot a few feet. "This should be connected inside you, which should make you untouchable when you're invisible."

"I'll put that in you, Vizzy," said Skinamar. He grabbed the black cube and opened the Invisi-Bot's thorax.

As he was rebuilding him, Martino showed the message plate to Zinger. Zinger grabbed it and twisted the small knob to an eighth of a centimeter, ready to play it.

"They said something about this sister of mine," said Martino.

"I believe she was kidnapped by the Sharp Empire that long time ago," said Zinger. He called Skinamar and the Invisi-Bot when Skinamar was done with the upgrade. Zinger placed the plate on the stick-built table and let the message play, releasing the knob:

"Zinger Warsp," the message began, showing the hologram of Mariana Izodorro, "Years ago, you fought in my father's alliance against evil. I believe his assassination was meant to protect my future. I'm chosen to face my execution. Please, please, I must have a rescuer." The message finished.

"Well," said Zinger. "The duty is complete."

"How did my parents die?" asked Martino.

"The Serpential emperor, Hieronymus Sharp," said Zinger, "who is a cobra with that of a lizard. He won the war against your parents' kingdom and he assassinated them."

And so, a team of heroes will be about to rise for freedom.

CHAPTER 7

KASSOW'S NEW PLANS

Meanwhile on the biosphere, the Death Scale, a meeting was planned in the Sharp Empire's home city of Serpentopolis, in the east building. The city was divided into four buildings: north, south, east, and west. They formed the shape of a rounded cross. In the middle was built the cobra head-shaped Palace of Sharp, where the emperor's throne room was located, and at the top is the eye of a serpent that is mechanical and electrical connected by two spires. This eye had ability to absorb the laser beams from the outer ends of each building and to make a larger laser beam for the Death Scale's firing sequence.

In the east building, which was about a mile long, (like I said, there was a meeting) Governor Kalvino Kassow had run an objective for the galactic warfare.

"Gentlemen," he started the meeting, "I have discovered our biosphere's abilities of destruction. We must authorize our enemies to sacrifice their declaration of freedom and prosperity."

Commander Karbono Kassow rose up and said, "When our enemies sacrifice, we shall conquer the galaxy instantly. This biosphere can have up to thirty quadrillion kilobytes for its frequency. Then victory belongs in our immortality."

"When our immortality vanishes for the Death Scale," said a Komodo dragon petty officer, "it will still automatically stand in the emperor's hands, according to his comments." He flicked his forked tongue as he finished his sentence.

"Victory shall be ours with better plans made along with the ones they've stolen," said the Serpential general, Karchong Fang, who is a powerful, four-armed, mammalian-reptilian beast with that of a gorilla and a tyrannosaurus. "Our tyranny cannot flee from our hands to our enemies'. When they underestimate our abilities, we shall deal with them."

The governor rose up and commanded, "We shall crush the Heaven Federation by one turn; our plans will automatically be simple and all that that implies."

Darth Waternoose was breathing heavily as he listened. Then he said, "The plans they had stolen will soon be back in our hands. The ability to destroy a certain fantasy is to make this biosphere fully operational."

"At least we've got the monitor repaired," said another komodo officer.

"Perhaps we should use that for our detection," said Waternoose.

"Don't try to fool us with your sorcery powers and philosophy, Lord Waternoose," the commander said in a rage. "We should already legalize our war against our enemies' ignorance. We have enough ways to locate the Heaven . . ." Waternoose choked him with the force in his sight. The commander hacked and gagged.

"I find your lack of agreement disturbing," said Waternoose.

The governor arose and shouted, "Enough of this! Waternoose, release him!"

"As you wish," said Waternoose, releasing the commander dropping his head on the table breathing heavily.

"All plans are getting to be successful," said the Serpential colonel, Croclaw, a crocodilian pirate knight with a left grappling three-fingered hand.

"Excellent," said the governor. "Lord Waternoose will advise us for the princess's execution." All of the officers left the conference room.

CHAPTER 8

DESTRUCTION HAPPENS

And so, back on Earth, in Ireland, Martino Izodorro, Skinamarinky-Dinky-Dink Skinamarinky-Doo, the Invisi-Bot, and Zinger Warsp were traveling until what they had not realized was destruction on a few certain parts of Earth. They were satisfied. They also noticed the leprechauns' collecting vehicle smoking as it was falling apart. Leprechaun corpses were lying around the wasteland.

"It looks like we're being qualified to war," said Zinger.

"I guess it was bad things having to come this way," said Skinamar.

"Maybe, something's trying to eliminate those who don't appease to somewhat madness," said Martino.

"I guess I should try to camouflage on this dirt," said the Invisi-Bot.

"Things are just getting me . . ." said Martino, "back . . . home." He dashed back to his uncle's truck.

"Wait, Marty!" Zinger called to him. "It's too dangerous!"

"I'll be careful!" Martino called back. He got into the truck and drove back to his aunt and uncle's farm.

"Hopefully, he'll be back," said Skinamar.

As Martino drove back home, he noticed that much of the island was burned and barren by bombs or grenades. Scale troopers were searching for prisoners and traitors.

When Martino got home, he walked towards his aunt and uncle's house shouting, "UNCLE ROWAN! AUNT MARA! UNCLE ROWAN!" He stopped. Then he saw the skeletons of his aunt and uncle. He suddenly realized that destruction was happening. Then he drove back to where his friends were waiting for him.

CHAPTER 9

A PLAN OF EXECUTION

So, back on the Death Scale, Darth Waternoose received a message from his creator, Emperor Sharp. The emperor's hologram appeared in Waternoose's wrist communicator.

"We must find the Heaven Federation's hidden base," said the emperor, flicking his forked tongue. "Princess Izodorro shall face her final fate for her family."

"She will tell the truth," said Waternoose, "or die."

The emperor's hologram vanished. Waternoose left the room he was in and called for his scale troopers. He led them to the detention level in the east building. The guards let them pass through the doorway to the detention halls. They stopped by the princess's cell. Waternoose opened the door. The princess awoke.

"And now, your highness, we will discuss the location of your Heavenly Federal base," said Waternoose. He had brought a floating robot, built by the emperor, called a psycholo-droid, which is used for reading the minds of innocent bystanders in hostage. It carried a shot with a liquid serum for if the princess took too long to answer. Waternoose used his top middle eye to look in a distance through the princess's head. Then he walked back through the doorway with his six crab-like legs folded under. Then he closed the door.

CHAPTER 10

HITCH A RIDE TO SPACE AND BEYOND

And now, flashbacking to Earth, Martino returned to his friends' current location by the leprechauns' broken down vehicle.

"I've heard that your aunt and uncle have been killed by the scale troopers," said Zinger, fluttering his wings as he moved towards Martino. "You could've been killed, too."

"I know," said Martino.

"Check this out," said Skinamar as he skipped to a pile of junk nearby. "I built this turbine motor for getting us out of here."

"Ah! Excellent, my ape friend!" exclaimed Zinger.

"If my calculations are correct," said the Invisi-Bot, "things are quite complicated."

The four friends hopped in the turbine vehicle. Martino started the engine.

"We must head down to Cork Harbor," Zinger instructed. "I have a launch pad there for taking us to the space station above."

When they traveled to the harbor, the turbine engine allowed them to get there fast. When they arrived at the harbor, a group of scale troopers shouted, "Halt!"

One of the troopers said, "You'll have a one way ticket to prison for drag racing down here on publicity. We must see your identification."

"You don't need to see his identification," said Zinger.

"We don't need to see his identification," said the trooper.

"These aren't the things you're looking for," said Zinger.

"These aren't the things we're looking for."

"Release us."

"Move along."

Martino was about to hit the gas pedal as Zinger said, "Hang on. I got a cover shield for an underwater trip." He pressed a button on the dashboard that put a solid plastic shield over the vehicle. Then they zoomed into the water.

As they were headed for the undersea launch pad, Martino wondered, "So how did you get us past those scale troopers? I thought we were dead."

"That's the force," said Zinger. "I flick it into the minds of those who would have been taught manners for what they see."

"Well, you can do your mental magic some other time, I suppose," said Skinamar.

All of a sudden, they saw a square prism tunnel, which led to the launch pad Zinger was talking about.

"You'll no longer be part of this planet, Marty," said Zinger as they traveled through the tunnel under green light, then yellow light.

The four friends suddenly ended up in an underwater room with an entrance hole in the ceiling, where the water level was affected by air pressure. Then they hovered to that surface. They hopped out of the vehicle and felt the air pressure of this underwater launch pad. When they walked up the yellow brick halls, they heard security voices call out: "Your identifications, please."

"Uh, Izodorro," said Martino, "Martino."

"What kind of animal are you?" the security asked.

"I'm a human!" Martino answered strongly with humor. "I've got a wasp, an orangutan, and a robot."

The security laughed hysterically. That took a minute until someone said, "You may enter your shuttle."

The four friends went up the spiral up-way, and then found a space shuttle underwater. They entered it then had to fasten seatbelts.

"This is going to be a long trip out of here, Marty," said Skinamar, "so don't panic."

"Seatbelts on?" said Zinger, standing in the pilot's seat and resting his front legs on the dashboard.

"We're good, I guess," said Martino. The encounter was activated. Zinger read them:

"9 . . . 8 . . . 7 . . . 6 . . . 5 . . . 4 . . . 3 . . . 2 . . . 1 . . . 0." The shuttle blasted off.

When the shuttle was about to rise to the surface, a ship full of leprechauns was floating until they saw bubbles below deck.

"ABANDON SHIP!" one of the leprechauns shouted. Then all leprechauns leaped into the water as the shuttle's fuel tank lifted the ship then it fell apart as it fell on the tips of the white rocket boosters and shuttle. The engines boiled the water with many bubbles.

Some of the leprechauns returned to the surface and one said, "Ya know, I've not seen one of those big rockets since I've seen a wee small child fly a toy plane."

"Yeah, that was surely a wee bit stupid," said another leprechaun.

The captain leprechaun rose to the surface and shouted, "I'll sue those blaggards for this!"

The shuttle continued to shoot into space, and then it left the atmosphere and entered a space station never seen before. When the four travelers entered the station, they noticed a gift shop, a restaurant, and an arcade room. Zinger buzzed into the gift shop for weapons to send to more heroes of the group about to rise. Martino, Skinamar, and the Invisi-Bot went into the arcade room. Martino was about to try out an arcade machine when he saw two male cubs, a fox and a cougar, were playing one.

"Can I have a turn after you, kids?" Martino asked.

"Sure," said the fox cub.

Martino had a strange thought about nature. He could realize that animals were talking to him. Just as the fox cub finished his game, Martino took his turn on the arcade machine with guns. He noticed the animation of aliens then he shot the screen by a bunch in a few seconds. The two cubs seemed doubtful.

"Since when do you shoot like that?" the fox cub asked in a rude way.

"Let's just leave him alone if he wants to cheat at everything," said the cougar cub. So the cubs left the arcade room.

Martino seemed tired of playing. He decided to leave as he noticed Skinamar and the Invisi-Bot had just left. Martino decided to find a table in the restaurant to rest. He couldn't think of leaving his home planet.

Then an average wolverine approached him and said, "Hey, man. Want to try this bottle zapper game with me?"

"No thanks. I'm good," said Martino. The wolverine remained standing by him for a second.

"Come on," he said, "even a baby can handle the job . . ."

"Fine," said Martino, getting up from the table he sat at. He followed the wolverine to the bottle zapper arcade pit. The wolverine sat in a middle chair while Martino sat next to him. They grabbed the laser cannons in front of themselves. The wolverine took his turn first keeping his aim on the three-yard distant bottle shelves then zapped some bottles one by one.

"See? Easy," said the wolverine, "give it a try."

Martino shot a bottle that fell backwards and knocked down a lot of bottles on the lower shelves. Then he zapped some more one by one.

"So where did you learn how to shoot like that?" the wolverine asked in surprise.

"A long story," Martino said.

Suddenly, Skinamar approached him saying, "Excuse me, sir, but he's with *us.*"

"Well alright then," said the wolverine, "I'll let you go."

Skinamar walked Martino to where Zinger and the Invisi-Bot were sitting. Alien musicians played their instruments on a nearby stage. They tweaked the tune of their song.

CHAPTER 11

MEET THE HEROES

When Martino and Skinamar walked to the table with Zinger and the Invisi-Bot, they met a male tiger with two females, a kangaroo and a foreign wolf from another planet. Martino and Skinamar took a seat with them.

"I'm Tiblo Tigro," said the tiger. "I'm captain of the Heaven Federation."

"Wow, good for you," said Martino. "Bu . . . , you're a tiger."

"That never stopped me or anyone else," said Captain Tiblo Tigro. He introduced his two maidens, "These are my maidens, Shana Cargon . . ." he pointed to the kangaroo. ". . . and Manda Monka," he pointed to the beautiful foreign wolf.

"Hi there," said Shana Cargon.

"Pleasure to meet you all," said Manda Monka.

"I'm Martino Izodorro," said Martino, "and this is Skinamarinky-Dinky-Dink Skinamarinky-Doo."

"Call me Skinamar," said Skinamar, as Martino pointed to him.

"I've got more gifts for you, freedom fighters," said Zinger. The next gifts were weapons for the other heroes and also instruments for use of calling for help. (I'll talk about those later)

Here is my note on the freedom fighters: Tiblo Tigro was once a fierce animal in the north of Asia. His family was once shot by poachers. The godly white condor, Artidector, was sent to take him to space for training. Tiblo was humanized. He was even told to hunt down the poachers who killed his family.

Shana Cargon is the mechanical maid of the team. As a joey, she was taught to do karate and she had created weapons for defending her herd, but was banished for her mistakes. Her parents were often part of a disadvantage and outplacement. But her intelligence could be useful. Artidector had found her lost.

Manda Monka came from the fourth planet from the star, Sirius. In the ancient city, half-submerged, her father, Genghis Monka, who was a count, was married to a fortune-teller named Moranis. As for their offspring, their elder daughter, Ninga, was crowned empress of that city. Their younger daughter, Manda, was chosen as a young swords girl. When war was declared in this city, Emperor Sharp electrocuted Count and Fortune-Teller Monka. He even bound and gagged their daughters. Ninga was anchored and drowned, but Manda was saved by Artidector.

So needless to say, a team of freedom fighters was born. Now back to the story . . .

"Is there a bathroom I can use?" Martino asked.

"Follow me," said Zinger. Martino followed him. Zinger led Martino to the co-restroom (explained in the introduction). Zinger then opened a stall, in which each door opened like elevator doors. Martino used the space toilet as Zinger confronted a robot holding diaper bags and urinal under trunks. The robot stood still by the restroom stalls as Zinger perched on its head, waiting for Martino. Just as Martino finished using the toilet, he found the robot with Zinger on it.

"This robot has these useful under goers," said Zinger, hovering, "try one of them on." He perched on the under trunks with urinal tubes.

"You want Styrofoam or black sponge?" asked the robot.

"I guess black sponge will be fine," said Martino. He took a pair of under trunks with black sponge-like fiber on the inside, and then he went back into the stall he used earlier to change.

When he was done putting on those trunks with the urine container taped on the front under his normal trousers, he left the restroom. Well, as he was about to, he confronted a short female feline soldier, who looked at him with amusement. Her name was Lei Sawyer. She always wore a skirt over her trousers.

"Oy," she said. "Just standing here for no reason?"

"I'm just leaving," said Martino.

"I'm Lei Sawyer," said the female feline. "Excuse me I need to change my diaper." She went into one of the stalls, having another pair of doors opening like elevator doors.

Martino returned to the table he sat at earlier. As he got there, Tiblo Tigro was testing the sound of the instrument he received from Zinger, the Tiger Horn.

"So," Tiblo said as Martino confronted him at the table, "what part of Earth are you from?"

"Ireland," said Martino.

"Wow," said Tiblo, "did any leprechauns traumatize you?"

"Totally," said Martino. "One time I had to get Skinamar back to the group, and a leprechaun shot a rock at my forehead with a slingshot harder than I thought."

"Well, you're lucky to be alive," said Tiblo.

CHAPTER 12

TRAINING, PART 1

All of a sudden, an alarm rang, shouting, "Jailbreak, jailbreak . . ." the alarm bell rang faster.

"We've got work to do now," said Tiblo. "Grab my paw." Martino did. Tiblo pressed a button on his wrist communicator that teleported him and Martino to wherever the jailbreak was happening.

When they found themselves in the cellar of the space station, a monstrous, hideous beast with the face of a lion, horns of a bull, and the rear end of a wolf, was roaming and finding a way out. It was running on power pipes. Tiblo and Martino readied their firearms.

"Turn left," Tiblo said, shooting a laser shot from one of his twin laser pistols, received from Zinger. The beast turned when he found the shot in the wall.

"I'll get him," said Martino. He shot his disk launchers toward the beast. The beast squatted when he witnessed the disks.

"Missed him," said Martino.

"We're not trying to hit him," said Tiblo. The two fighters headed for the beast's direction.

"Make him turn right!" shouted Tiblo. Martino kept firing and firing at the wall ahead. The beast turned right.

"If you can't do it with one shot at a time, don't do it at all," said Tiblo. He pressed a button on his wrist communicator, holding it for his message, saying, "Bring the net."

Then suddenly, a hatch on the ceiling opened and lowered a rubber wire net for a trap for the beast. The beast headed for a slope with a drain that poured sewage water. He tried to leap over it, but Tiblo shot the drain to block the beast's path. The beast fell on the pouring sewage, then slipped and fell in the waiting net. The net zoomed back up to its place.

"Mission accomplished," said Tiblo. "Come, Marty."

Martino grabbed his paw as Tiblo pressed the teleportation button on his wrist communicator. He and Martino teleported back to the restaurant table they sat at. Suddenly, a roaring sound of the beast emerged in the detention hall. Soldiers were knocked and whacked away by the beast. Tiblo and Martino went with Zinger to the detention hall by the restaurant. As they walked there, the beast threw a soldier out of the doorway of the captivity room. Tiblo and Martino entered the room. Neither male nor female could hold the beast under control.

"Mister Beast," said Tiblo. "You've done illegal things lately." The beast turned his head to him. Tiblo continued his statement, "For your temper is uncontrollable, . . . you want to go home, don't you."

"Home," said the beast. "Home's with hostage if that's what they say."

"By what name do you prefer?" Tiblo asked.

"They call me Rufus," said the beast. "There's no reason to be afraid."

Martino walked forward a few inches and said, "Who says I'm afraid?"

"NONE OF YOUR CONCERN!" the beast yelled. Martino skipped back.

"*You stink of fear!*" the beast growled. "You wait to see my real ego." He huffed and puffed in a rampage. His muscles and fur shrunk and vanished. The beast changed into a human with blonde hair and he could use another suit.

"Regulto Beauxon," he said, "at your service." He broke free from the cords that held him.

"We'll take him," said Tiblo. And so, Regulto was the last member to join the freedom fighter team.

Regulto Beauxon was half British and half French, according to his parents (British father and French mother). He was a self-meditator for his fear. He invented a medicine that he thought would make him brave, but a force from the constellation of Leo the lion turned him into that beast form that conquered his fear for him.

As the freedom fighters walked out of the captivity room with Regulto Beauxon, Zinger gave him a weapon.

The freedom fighters readied themselves for a combat demonstration.

"At least you two could count as good partners there, eh," said Zinger to Tiblo and Martino.

"At least we got Skinamar, too," said Martino.

"It's time for a battle demo!" exclaimed Zinger, hovering up toward the switch that opened the door for the training stage. "Ready your firearms and get set . . . go!" He activated the switch. The door opened like a garage gate. The six freedom fighters aimed their weapons for the appearing targets, which were pirate knights, scale troopers and alien monsters. Skinamar used his sun ray phaser that burned some pieces of the targets to a crisp. When Shana Cargon activated her firearms they used a lot of air pressure like a fan or a blow dryer that caused them to launch boomerangs (those weapons are known as "Boomerang Launchers"). The boomerangs bounced at multiple targets everywhere. Manda Monka's weapon was a steel crossbow that shot arrows that fly fast, they could go through walls. Regulto's weapon appeared to be a cannon-like bazooka shooting spherical steel balls. As usual, Martino fired his disk launchers and Tiblo used his twin blasters.

As the demonstration was over, the lights behind the stage turned on, there appeared to be a large red ship with all types of fins of a fish.

"What a dump," said Martino.

Tiblo dashed in front of the team, introducing the ship, saying, "Behold, the Great Red Shark; the sturdiest ship in the fleet!" The team walked aboard as Zinger buzzed in. The conveyor belt lifted and moved back into its slot. Everyone was ready for the trip. The entrance door closed. The ship had two decks.

"Next stop, Neverland," said Zinger. "I sense that's where our enemies have now headed for."

The Great Red Shark flew out of the space station. Tiblo activated the switch for the hyper-drive. The ship then vanished in the distance.

CHAPTER 13

THE WEAPON TEST

And so, Zinger was right about the enemy forces. The Death Scale had traced the direction from Big Ben in London, England to the second star to the right (according to the fairy tale of Peter Pan) using Serpentopolis's mechanical serpent's eye. As they were about to test the laser devices in the palace's basement, Darth Waternoose walked down there to converse with Governor Kassow.

"We've asked the princess about our enemy's location," Waternoose started, "except she is reluctant to betray her allies."

"I'll take care of that," said the governor, tapping his beak. Then the scale troopers brought Princess Mariana Izodorro forward to him and Waternoose.

"Governor Kassow," said the princess, "you should not have been reading my mind about the way I reclined on my dreams."

"Charming," said the governor. "Indeed you'll have accepted the truth about your philosophy, your underestimation towards us, and all that that implies." Waternoose nodded his head slowly.

The governor began his word, "Now, princess, before your execution, we should discuss this one thing very thoroughly; since you are reluctant to tell us where your Heavenly Federal friends are, we shall without any choice test our ultimate weapon on this infernal fantasy world of Neverland." Neverland was about to be viewed on the giant computer screen.

"No," said the princess. "Many Earthly children always believed in Neverland, it was their fondest dream, you can't legally . . ."

"Now you hold your tongue!" the governor interrupted. "When I say we are without a choice, I mean to say we have no choice but to do what the emperor tells us. He has powers to legalize and illegalize everything he wants or not. And once our biosphere turns out fully operational then we shall name the system or nebula." He began to turn in anger. "And now I grow tired of waiting for one answer from you; where is the Heavenly Federal base?! . . . and don't lie to me."

The princess rolled her eyes with her mouth half open. "Oz," she finally said, "the wonderful land of Oz."

"You see, Lord Waternoose," said the governor, "she can be reasonable."

"She will have more manners to learn," said Waternoose.

"Father," the governor's son, the commander called him, "we have Neverland in range."

"You may fire when ready," said the governor.

"*What??*" the princess was shocked.

"You heard me your highness," said the governor, "we have no choice but to do what the emperor tells us."

"*No!*" the princess shouted. She tried to run and stop the officers, but Waternoose quickly reached and grabbed her by the shoulders, holding her close to him.

The officers activated the keys, levers, buttons and switches for the Death Scale's firing system. The princess watched hopelessly. Suddenly, the spires at the far end of each building shot laser beams toward the mechanical eye. The eye absorbed them, and then shot a larger beam at Neverland. And so that world was no more.

"Think about whose side you are on, your highness," said Waternoose. "Ours . . . or theirs?" He pointed to the giant computer screen showing Neverland's nebular extinction.

The Serpential sergeant, Hawkeye, who is a long-beaked bird of prey with a mechanical left eye for zooming a sight for distance, flew down and formed his feet into a grapple around the princess's neck, nearly choking her. Then he lowered his feet.

"That's what we do to those who take too long to answer," he said.

The governor walked toward the princess. Then he said, "And this is what we do to those who answer with a lie." He whacked her on the head with the solid, stainless steel ball top of his walking stick. "Take her back to her cell," he commanded the scale troopers.

"Yes, sir," one of the troopers said as they walked the princess back to her detention cell.

And so, Waternoose decided to make modifications for the princess's execution.

CHAPTER 14

TRAINING, PART 2

Meanwhile, the Great Red Shark continued its voyage around and amongst stars and planets; in the ship there are two decks with forty-eight seats.

In the lower deck behind all seat aisles, there was a plenty empty space for more battle/combat training. Martino was told to test his skills with a steel club on red light pillars. He used his reflexes on each pillar that lit beside, in front, and behind him, smacking them with the club.

"You're very good," said Zinger. "Let's give you a little challenge on this combat test." He grabbed a ring-like clipping object, and then buzzed toward Martino to clip the ring over his eyes. It was a plastic clipping blindfold (or blind clip).

"Ugh!" Martino cried as Zinger put the clip on his face. "With one of these things on, I can't even see."

"Just remember where the posts are without looking," said Zinger. "Wait for the sounds."

Martino listened for beeping sounds of the lampposts. Then he heard one and whacked it, then another and another, according to Zinger's instructions.

"See?" said Zinger. "You can do it."

Martino took off the blind clip and said, "At least I didn't have to remember, I just listen."

Zinger took the blind clip then buzzed over toward Shana, who was throwing steel-pointed iron spears at a large target.

"Excellency comes toward you by every instant," said Zinger to Shana. "Let's do a challenge test with this." He snapped the blind clip behind the back of her head, placing it in front of her eyes.

"I hate blindfolds," she said, having issues.

"Just relax," said Zinger, "remember where the target is from your current position."

So Shana remembered her sight of the target, and then threw the spears one by one. She took off the blind clip and noticed a bull's eye.

"See?" said Zinger. "Easy."

Author's note: You might imagine such good fighters in this story. Those who are well-trained would just be automatically able to fight.

Meanwhile, Skinamar and the Invisi-Bot were playing a game of a monster chessboard table, which is different than regular chess. This chessboard is round, in which different types of monsters can move in any segment that makes the shape of a circle. Zinger buzzed toward them.

"Fighting a monster is a dangerous task," he said. "It takes more than brute strength to conquer one." So his thought went on for a long time for he knew that a monster would conquer all sorts of heroes.

CHAPTER 15

THE HENCHMONSTERS

On the Death Scale, the emperor's monsters inhabit and conquer the biosphere. Specific inhabitants are under their control.

The monsters in these secret worlds include:

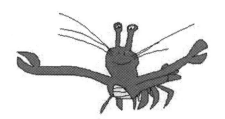

Lava Lobster: a lobster volcanologist with fiery powers.

Monstrous Slug: a slug with an embodied leech giving quantum education to children.

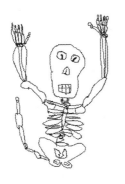

Junky the Bulldog: a dog that likes garbage.

Long-Tailed Skeleton: a human skeleton with a long tail.

Clown Coach: an evil clown with a hypno-whistle.

Three Heads: a three-headed poison ivy lizard.

Scorpionyx: a large, mighty, tank-hard scorpion.

Grop: a green blob of slime that grows plants.

The Jamba Juice Glob: A blob built up of many fruit juices.

Sparxcalibur: an electrical giant.

Mega Hawk: a hawk with hypnotic and nuclear powers.

Tri-Psy-PO: a one-eyed, tripedal robot with a hypnotic eye.

Plag: a black skeleton of plague.

Brocker: a hunchback beast with brutal strength.

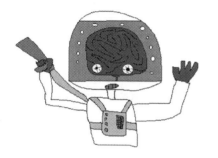

Ice Brain: a robot with a brain glass and an ice blaster with a pack.

Stargoyle: a black gargoyle that causes hurricanes.

These are the first sixteen monsters to face.

There are other monsters on the three planets that follow the Death Scale as it moves. The monsters have many unique abilities. They might team up when a battle is planned.

Now back to the story, the emperor had a conversation with his henchmonsters in holograms.

"We have an enemy force," said the emperor, "defend our biosphere with all your might." He flicked his forked tongue.

"We shall roast them," said Lava Lobster who had a strange accent.

"We shall slime the minds of those who don't know better," said Monstrous Slug.

"I'll teach them manners by clowning around," said Clown Coach.

"Their bones shall rattle like mine," said Long-Tailed Skeleton.

"We'll poison them," said Three Heads.

"They shall face a new great plague," said Plag.

"We shall do our best," said all the monsters.

"Defend our biosphere," said the emperor again. Then all of the monsters' holograms vanished.

Just then, General Karchong Fang entered the throne room through the elevator. He folded his four arms.

"We've repaired the monitor, your highness," he told the emperor.

"Excellent," said the emperor. He pressed a button on the front of one of the arms of his throne, the communicator button. "Bring in Waternoose," he said through it.

Meanwhile, the Death Scale moved toward the sphincter portal to the Land of Oz.

"Nearly entering the Land of Oz," said the monitor, "the Heavenly Federal base appears nowhere in this world."

Governor Kassow and Darth Waternoose tested their memory of the princess's words.

"A lie!" said the governor, turning to Waternoose. "She lied to us."

"I told you she has been reluctant to betray her allies," said Waternoose. "She remains on their side."

And so, the execution was planned.

CHAPTER 16

LANDING ON THE DEATH SCALE

Meanwhile, back in outer space, the team of freedom fighters headed for the last location of Neverland. Tiblo Tigro called out, "People, we're coming up on Neverland." He stopped the hyper drive. Then he noticed the surrounding of star gases. "No sign of it," he said. "It's totally blown away."

"What?!" Martino shouted, leaping out of his seat. "How?" He ran to the pilot's chamber from the upper deck's left aisle.

"It was the Sharp Empire," said Zinger. "Their ultimate weapon has enough power to destroy whatever worlds happen in stories."

They passed through the nebula. A strange ship flew in front of the Great Red Shark.

"Hey, that's a strange-looking ship," said Martino. The ship flew ahead of them fast. "It's heading for that green and tan lone moon."

"That's your imagination," said Tiblo.

"That's no moon," said Zinger. "It's a biosphere."

"Same thing sometimes," said Tiblo. "Let's see if I can get us away from here." He tried steering the Shark out of sight, but the Death Scale's orbit dragged the ship with many forces of gravity toward its surface. "I can't . . . get us out of . . . here!" He wrestled with the steering handle on the dashboard.

"We're still heading towards it!" said Martino.

All of a sudden, the force of gravity made them land on the Death Scale. Tiblo steered the ship into an open hatch at the far end of the south building of Serpentopolis. Just as he landed the ship steadily in the hangar, a group of scale troopers surrounded the ship. The freedom fighters hid in secret hatches inside the ship. The entrance hatch lowered the conveyor and the scale troopers entered it.

"We have an enemy ship that has approached our city," one of the troopers said through his wrist communicator. The troopers maneuvered through the halls and decks, detecting the ship's passengers.

"There's no one here," a trooper said. They all walked off the ship. The freedom fighters opened the hatch to check if the coast was clear. And so, they were safe.

Meanwhile, on the detention level, silk and rubber robed guards grabbed Princess Mariana Izodorro out of her cell for her execution. They bound her wrists and ankles then gagged her. Then they brought her to the Serpential officers.

Back in the south building's hangar, scale troopers were standing guard in front of the Great Red Shark. Tiblo called to some of them, "Hey, you down there!" Two troopers heard him. "Could you give us a hand with this?!" Tiblo called them again. The troopers walked up in the ship. Tiblo shot them and knocked their helmets off. Then he and Martino took the suits off of their scaly bodies.

"RG-548, what's going on?" a Serpential officer called through a loud speaker in a nearby security tower. "RG-548, do you copy?" Suddenly, droids came by to carry the damaged lizards out of the Great Red Shark. The security officer looked out the window and saw the lizards being carried away by the droids. He walked out of his security tower room to see what was going on. Tiblo and Martino walked out of the ship disguised as scale troopers (Martino had the trooper suit's tail tunnel drag behind him). The security officer ran up the hallway to get help. Tiblo flicked his finger forward to call the rest of the team. They all headed for the security tower room. Tiblo and Martino took off their disguise helmets.

As they walked in the room, Tiblo had a decision to make. As he thought of it, Zinger warned the team, "Now, I want you all to stay cautious of security elements in the city. The Death Scale contains many dangers."

"Where are you going, Zinger?" asked Martino.

"I'm going to shut down the weapon's power," said Zinger. As he headed for the door, he said, "Remember, the force will be with you; always." Then he flew out the door and closed it.

Martino walked toward the Invisi-Bot, who was by the room's locator map screen of Serpentopolis.

"What *is* this, anyway?" Martino asked.

"This biosphere is called, the Death Scale," said the Invisi-Bot. "It is also the Sharp Empire's ultimate weapon. It is used to destroy those imaginary worlds that mainly exist in fairy tales and most beloved stories. There is also a control device inside the biosphere preparing it to leave its current position. There are many strange places on this biosphere, so let's all be cautious."

"Hold on," said Martino. "About my sister . . ."

"Oh yes," said the Invisi-Bot. "She is being held for an execution today."

"Oh no," said Martino. "This is horrible. If we don't save her in time, all laws will be broken!"

"Don't worry," Tiblo stopped him. "Not everyone lasts that long, especially with laws."

"But they're gonna kill her!" Martino shouted.

"Better her than me!" Tiblo snapped.

"My mother, Moranis, once said that execution was as cruel as murder," said Manda Monka.

"Although it is," said Skinamar, "deaths are all planned out for each opponent."

"I have an idea," said Martino. "Invisi-Bot, hand me those binders over there." The Invisi-Bot gave the brass binders to him from the security control panel. Martino walked towards Regulto who was standing by the door.

"I'm gonna put these on you," he said when he was about to bind Regulto's wrists.

"Uh . . ." Regulto spoke out stepping back, "I don't think so. That would be a betrayal."

"It is no betrayal," a monstrous growling voice spoke out behind him. It was Rufus the Beast.

"How would *you* know what he's doing?" Regulto spoke back. He saw the reflection of his beast self.

"Trust him, never fear," said the beast reflection.

Regulto nodded his head, his mouth mostly open. Then he turned back to Martino.

"Uh, y-you put those on him," Martino said, handing the binders to Tiblo. Tiblo walked towards Regulto, who raised his fists in front of himself.

"Don't worry, Reg," Tiblo said binding his wrists. "I'm sure he knows what he has in mind." Then he turned to the others, saying, "Now, while we are gone, I want the rest of you to stay quiet. If anyone comes by, hide in that closet over there." He pointed to a polygonal part of the room at the side of the window. The rest of the team remained. And so, Tiblo, Martino, and Regulto exited the room, putting on their scale trooper helmets.

Meanwhile, Zinger snuck through the Serpentopolis halls, hovering and fluttering his wings. He snatched onto the ceiling, avoiding the troopers and officers, walking down the hallways. Then he buzzed into a nearby hole that led him through a clear, plastic tunnel that headed for the basement of the Palace of Sharp.

Now, back to Tiblo and Martino, disguised in scale trooper suits with Regulto bound, they walked through the hallways, finding the detention level. Suddenly, a small robot sped in front of them. It flashed a blue sparkling light in front of them to create holograms. This robot is known as a communica-droid. The robot sped to the emperor to show the holograms of the true identities under the scale trooper suits. Tiblo, Martino, and Regulto walked onto an elevator that led to the detention level in the east building. As they rode the elevator, the binders on Regulto's wrists loosened. Tiblo tested the tightness that goes around.

"This is definitely not gonna work," he said.

"Why didn't you say so before?" asked Martino.

"I *did* say so before," Tiblo said.

Meanwhile, in the Palace of Sharp, the guards brought Princess Mariana Izodorro, gagged with wrists and ankles bound, forward to the emperor. Officers and pirate knights stood in front of the throne. Since the governor remembered the lie, he walked toward the princess, saying, "Your lies have brought you to your fate." He whacked her on the head with the stainless steel ball top of his walking stick a second time.

The emperor called a ship through the speaker on the arm of his throne.

"We shall drown her in Lake Prisoner," he said to his followers. Suddenly, the communica-droid from the halls showed the holograms it recorded.

"Ah! Yes," said the emperor. "The freedom fighters of the Heaven Federation are here, but they're too late." And then, the ship he called for hovered in front of the large window behind the throne. The emperor opened the centerpiece of the window with his force powers, using his hands. Then he, the officers, and the pirate knights took the princess aboard for her execution. Then the ship flew to Lake Prisoner, which is a low lake south of Serpentopolis.

CHAPTER 17

IT'S TOO LATE

Just as Tiblo, Martino, and Regulto went to the detention level, they stood behind two lizards, sitting in front of a long dashboard.

"Where are you taking this human?" asked one of the lizards.

"We're taking him into an available cell," said Tiblo.

"This is not the time for another detention," said the lizard, "the emperor hasn't called for one."

Suddenly, Rufus the Beast's voice appeared in Regulto's head, saying, "Never fear." Then Regulto broke free from the binders in rage.

"LOOK OUT! HE'S LOOSE!" shouted Tiblo. He fired his blasters toward the detention hallway.

"What are you doing?!" shouted the lizard.

Tiblo took off his disguise helmet to show his face. "I'm here to manipulate your detained enemies," he said.

The two lizards ran into the elevator to call security. One pressed the down button then they waited. Martino headed down the hallway in search of this sister's cell. The communicator buzzed.

"Keep going, Marty, I'll handle this call," said Tiblo. Regulto reclined on the wall. Tiblo pressed the communicator button then answered, "We're all fine. The enemy just raged out of sight. Uh, negative, negative, our enemy's gone to detain himself."

"Wait a second," said the voice through the communicator, "who is this? What is your operating number?"

Tiblo grabbed one of his blasters and shot the communicator, smoking parts of the dashboard.

Suddenly, an alarm voice rang out, "Emergency! Emergency! Enemy witness must be eliminated!"

"MARTY, WE'RE BEING TERMINATED!" Tiblo called to Martino.

Martino checked all cells, but no sign of his sister.

Meanwhile, back to the rest of the team in the security room by the hangar, Manda Monka had to change her diaper in the polygonal room. Suddenly, a band of troopers arrived by the whole room's doorway. The team went into the polygonal room to hide. Manda had to dress herself back in her battle dress.

"Stay calm," commanded Skinamar. "I have no idea what they are looking for."

"Perhaps us," said Manda. She headed into the garbage chute.

"Bad idea!" shouted Skinamar. Manda slid in the chute. Skinamar dashed toward it. "MANDA!" he shouted into it. "Oh well," he said, taking his head out of the chute. "It's just us."

Suddenly, a communication beeped on the Invisi-Bot's wrist. He answered it.

"Guys," it was Martino, "I went to the princess's cell and she wasn't there."

"She's facing her fate already, I suppose," said the Invisi-Bot. "We're too late!"

"Great!" said Martino turning off his wrist communicator.

Suddenly, scale troopers emerged into the detention halls firing their machine guns. Tiblo aimed one of his blasters at a vent then shot it.

"Quick, into the garbage chute!" he called Martino and Regulto.

They all headed into the garbage vent. As they leaped into it, they fell into large piles of scrap metal, molded gut food, and monsters' junk. There also appears to be glass and broken mechanical parts. Anyway, having stealth, the three heroes walked around. Regulto found the exit door.

"I've found the way out!" he called to Tiblo and Martino.

Tiblo and Martino walked forward to the side of the room where green and orange waste water poured out of a pipe on the upper wall. They found Manda.

"Manda!" shouted Tiblo. "How did *you* get in here?"

"Fine time to excrete," said Manda. "Troopers were coming so *I'm* trying to hide!"

"Well, you've come to the right place," said Martino. A noise occurred throughout the garbage room. It had screeches of rubbing metal and bubbling liquid.

". . . or not," said Tiblo.

Suddenly, a hatch opened below the sewage water and a bundle of bubbles headed for the piled garbage's shore. A hideous, snake-like monster rose above the sewage surface. It had a scallop-shaped head with four slit eyes, hollow nostrils, razor-sharp teeth, and a sturdy forked tongue. It made a loud gurgling scream. Tiblo shot one of his blasters at its muzzle. The garbage monster hissed and screamed. It grabbed a piece of scrap metal from the shore then it ate it. It crawled out of the water and chased after the heroes. Martino and Manda ran for the exit where Regulto was. Tiblo kept shooting the garbage monster in the open mouth. The monster grew angrier. Suddenly, it jumped into the air and opened its jaws about to eat Tiblo. He evaded the monster with a back flip. The monster fell into a hole between it and Tiblo. Tiblo fell backward into a bare sewage puddle. Manda ran toward him saying, "Are you alright? What happened?"

"Don't worry," said Tiblo. "It's gone."

Meanwhile, Regulto stood by the door knocking for a minute. Then Rufus the Beast showed himself in a nearby broken mirror, saying, "You will need your medicine."

"Except I left it back on the ship," said Regulto. Suddenly, another noise began to emerge from the ceiling. It began to fall slowly onto the heroes from far above.

"REGULTO!" yelled Tiblo. "You better not have touched anything over there!"

"I *didn't!*" Regulto called back. "I was just looking for the switch that opens this door!"

"I got it!" called Martino. He dug into his trooper disguise's backpack. He found a pick axe-like object. "Come on, there's gotta be something better than this!" He kept digging and accidentally activated a disk-shaped bomb. He pulled it out. "That'll work," he said. He ran to the door where Regulto tried to pry it open. Martino placed the bomb, sticking it on the central emblem. "Back away," he grabbed Regulto and ran from the doorway.

The bomb beeped faster and faster for a few seconds, until it finally exploded. The door fell backward. The way out was made. The heroes finally escaped. As they walked out of the garbage room, Martino made contact with the rest of the team.

"Invisi-Bot," he said through the mouth piece of his communicator, "have you got any idea of the princess's current location?"

The Invisi-Bot answered, "She is already being executed over Lake Prisoner."

"Oh great," said Martino. The heroes ran back to the hangar.

Meanwhile, Zinger buzzed into the lower cellar and found the volume switches of the Death Scale's frequency of laser power. They were nailed on a hollow tower with four giant electric tubes of power that ran towards the outer end of the bottom of each building of Serpentopolis. Zinger flew toward the tower to turn down the Death Scale's weapon volume. As he did, a loud humming sound emerged and lowered as he pulled down the clicking handles. The volume reached down to one. Then he flew to an upper tunnel, which led to the bowels of the Palace of Sharp.

Meanwhile, Darth Waternoose made contact with the twin vulture viceroys, Hooker and Blunt Volton, while the transportation headed for Lake Prisoner.

"We've located our intruders," said Hooker.

"The force is with them all," said Waternoose. "Exterminate them wherever you locate them."

"Yes, sir," said the viceroys.

Back in the hangar bay, Shana, Skinamar, and the Invisi-Bot waited for the other four heroes to return as they were guarded by scale troopers. As they reunited, Tiblo chased the troopers away with his blasters. Just as they found their ship's current landing spot, it was gone.

And so, they found a disk in the middle of the floor. Martino picked it up and pressed a button on the side. It showed his sister's execution. Pirate knights were herding her off the ledge of the ship they were on. As the princess stepped toward the ledge, General Fang swung his fist across the back of her head, then the princess began to fall into Lake Prisoner, her wrists and ankles bound and a gag in her mouth. She was chained to a heavy steel ball that pulled her down to the lake's floor. She was shaking and swimming, but she was unable to break free. Water started to run into her boots and her diaper. This appeared to be the fate of Princess Mariana Izodorro; and so she drowned. Suddenly, a metal wall, surrounding the bottom of the lake, opened its doors. A swarm of robots headed toward the princess, lying on the brown sandy floor. Then they began to create an ice crystal to hold the princess. As they froze her inside, they hovered and rose toward the surface. They hovered all the way into the sky. As they did, the emperor jogged toward the edge of the ship then jumped. Then suddenly, he spread his cape into the form of a wing span. He flew up to the sky where the robots were holding the frozen princess. The emperor shot lightning out of his fingertips to give the robots an ability to form an electrical wire net to hold the princess in the Death Scale's sky like a satellite.

As the freedom fighters watched the holograms in the hangar, Martino had another strange feeling.

"I'm definitely too late," he said.

"Don't worry!" a voice came from a tunnel in the ceiling far above. It was Zinger. "For all of you who missed your next flight, there is a special task for a team of freedom fighters. We can find the Great Red Shark from whoever stole it, and when we do, we shall meet our celestial friend, Artidector." He lowered himself down to the team, perching on the floor. Tiblo turned off the hologram message player. Then Zinger went up to the top of the security tower to grab a long cord with a handle on one end and a hook on the other.

CHAPTER 18

THE TEST OF COMBAT

Zinger brought the rubber hooking cord down to the freedom fighters. He had them grab onto the rubber body length.

"Follow me," he said. "We have a battle to do." As the freedom fighters held on tight to the cord one by one, Zinger lifted it by the handle end within his jointed legs and hovered into the air. Making sure it was high enough, the freedom fighters readied themselves; then they rose. Zinger flew the team out of the doorway of the hangar bay.

"Are you really that strong enough?!" Martino called up to Zinger.

"I'm an intelligent insect!" said Zinger. "I've become more powerful than any humans imagined!"

Just as he lowered the team, he witnessed the frozen crystal containing the princess. The emperor flew back to the ship he was transported on with his foot soldiers and officers. Zinger gained a horrid emotion throughout his body. All of a sudden, the freedom fighters heard rumbles throughout the landscape. The emperor's henchmonsters arrived.

"Welcome to our world!" they all said. They decided to lead the freedom fighters to the Therapsid Jungle, which was in the middle of the front part of the Death Scale. As they stopped there, a plan was being made. Clown Coach blew his whistle toward the wild creatures of the jungle. Lava Lobster and Monstrous Slug stood guard of the freedom fighters. Lava Lobster flicked his antennae; then he plunged his pincers into the ground, creating volcanic geysers a few yards away from himself. The freedom fighters fled the fire, except for Tiblo and Manda.

"Turn around!" Lava Lobster commanded. Tiblo followed his instruction.

"You too, mademoiselle," Lava Lobster commanded Manda.

Suddenly, Monstrous Slug shot the embodied leech from the back of his throat; then grabbed Tiblo at the back of his head, pulling toward his mouth. He used his mental ability to check his memory of joy or enjoying things from years of youth. Tiblo had no such memories. Monstrous Slug released him.

"This tiger's had a normal life," he said. "Now as for the she-wolf . . ." he was about to check Manda's memories, but all of a sudden, Skinamar activated his instrument, the chimpanzee's klaxon.

"Who dares disturb the guardian?!" Monstrous Slug gurgled.

Zinger lowered himself next to Skinamar.

"Not you again!" shouted Lava Lobster.

Junky the Bulldog barked. Clown Coach led a gaggle of hypnotized monkey lizards to jump on and wrestle Martino. Martino could not resist.

"Well now, earthly human," said Clown Coach, "are you in or out?"

"I cannot resist," said Martino, panicking. He tried shaking off the lizards. Some were knocked away, but some hooked onto his pilot's outfit. Suddenly, Tiblo emerged from Lava Lobster's fire square and shot the monkey lizards off of Martino.

"You ever touch my human friend again, you'll have to pay the forfeit," he scolded to Clown Coach.

"As you wish," said Clown Coach. "ATTACK!"

The monsters readied themselves for battle. Long-Tailed Skeleton shivered his bones. Monstrous Slug drooled slime. Three Heads wagged his tail and rocked his heads back and forth. The fight began.

"Brace yourselves!" cried Zinger. He grabbed coconuts from palm trees around. He dropped them on some of the monsters' heads. Monstrous Slug opened his jaws in front of Tiblo who blocked the bite with a stick. Monstrous Slug bit hard to snap the stick. Lava Lobster used his pincers to burn the trunks down to the core to make them fall. Three Heads planted poison ivy by spitting into holes in the ground. These six henchmonsters raged the jungle every square yard.

And so, the six freedom fighters escaped the rampage.
The next roadblock was a river. It contained a cold liquid
element with many amounts of cold steam emancipating
through the air.

"Is this even . . . ?" Martino wondered.

"No," Tiblo answered. "It's liquid nitrogen." The river
was of course known as the "Nitro River".

"How come you're the one who knows this stuff?"
asked Shana in a way with issues.

"I'm the captain, I know everything," said Tiblo.

"How are we supposed to cross this river?" asked
Manda.

"Good question," said Skinamar. "Watch this." He
stretched one of his arms to a distant rubber tree on the
other side. Then he zoomed through the air and across the
river. He accidentally smacked himself in the face when he
hit the tree. He slid down the tree. Then he looked around
and found a control panel a few yards south. He skipped
towards it and took a look. The text said "Nitro River"
in atomic letters. Then he found two buttons; one said
"Plant tree east" while the other said "Plant tree west". He
pressed the "Plant tree west" button, noticing the three-
dimensional diagram of the river on the control panel. The
rubber tree lowered itself into the ground and arose on the
other side of the river.

"I'm first," said Tiblo. He grabbed the top of the tree,
pulling the whole thing towards himself and hooking
his boots around the base. As he unhooked, he began to
release himself soaring high into the air.

"Way to go, tiger!" Skinamar called out.

As Tiblo landed on the other side with Skinamar, the rest of the crew, one at a time, grabbed the tree and leaped to the other side. As they all came back together, the next part of combat began. More henchmonsters arose: Scorpionyx, Grop, the Jamba Juice Glob, Sparxcalibur, Mega Hawk, and Brocker. They grouped together as they utilized their powers.

"Taste this blast!" said Scorpionyx, shooting a bullet of his laser poison.

Tiblo snuck under his body to his metasoma's base. Then Mega Hawk screeched and made a giant, purple, egg-shaped grenade and dropped it. Tiblo dashed back to the team as the grenade exploded. Purple gas spread everywhere. Suddenly, behind the team arose the Jamba Juice Glob.

"Ha ha!" the glob laughed. "Now you're all stuck with me, the Jamba Juice Glob."

Skinamar felt delighted. He began to lick and drink some juice from the glob. The glob shriveled and oozed away from the freedom fighters. Suddenly, green slime oozed behind them, then around them. It was Grop. He splattered around the heroes, growing thorn vines to form a cage around them. All of a sudden, Sparxcalibur and Brocker planned their attacks. Sparxcalibur created a swarm of lightning bolts.

"End of the line, Heavenly Federal freedom fighters!" he shouted launching his lightning.

Brocker growled and shook his Ankylosaurus-like head. He shone his four red eyes, showing his anger. Then he ran and grabbed a giant boulder. Just as he was about to throw it at the heroes, a bright white glow appeared in the sky, lowering toward the Death Scale. The monsters ran away. A pair of wings spread out of the glow. It could be a god. But it appears to be a giant bird. It was Artidector.

CHAPTER 19

MEET ARTIDECTOR

Despite the stories of the Heaven Federation, Artidector was always around to help heroes with revival powers. And so, Artidector landed on the Death Scale to give the freedom fighters more than brute strength.

"Welcome, freedom fighters," he said. "Welcome back, Captain Tiblo Tigro, Shana Cargon, and Manda Monka. Welcome, Skinamarinky-Dinky-Dink Skinamarinky-Doo. Welcome Martino Izodorro and Regulto Beauxon. I have been authorized to give you the power to overcome the Sharp Empire. Come into my shack." He led the freedom fighters into his white hut, which was as tall as a redwood tree. He began to grant more abilities for the heroes to go beyond obstacles and amongst them.

After that power up for strength and ability to overcome the Serpential forces, Martino stood out on the Death Scale's grass in front of Artidector's hut, feeling guilty for letting his sister die in her execution by the Sharp Empire. Artidector flew toward him and stood next to him.

"I can't believe I had to let the enemy execute my sister," said Martino. "They seem impossible to defeat."

"Martino," said Artidector, "I will do anything to help your sister. She will have to wait a long time to breathe once again. My powers of revival are not legal for a while. I must find my children."

"Marty!" called Tiblo. He ran towards Martino and Artidector. He had a message, "The Great Red Shark is located."

"Finally," said Martino.

Suddenly, a figure came the distance. It was Zinger carrying the Invisi-Bot from being left behind. As they landed, the Invisi-Bot could barely get up.

"Thank you for leaving me far behind," he said. "I just had to modify your luck being with our . . . old . . . friend," he noticed Artidector.

"Long time no see," said Artidector.

"Just a well being of an insect," said Zinger.

Tiblo and Martino walked toward Artidector, waiting for their turn to talk. Artidector turned down to them.

"How's my stuff?" Tiblo asked.

"I am making new individual fighter ships for you and your crew," said Artidector.

Meanwhile, away from that point, the rest of the team had cleaned the Great Red Shark and waxed it. As they waited for Artidector's next surprise, Skinamar had to organize the decks of the ship. Manda went for other modifications. She swept a hedge away with her paws and a bipedal lizard pirate knight appeared. He scared Manda way. Suddenly, more pirate knights leaped out of their hiding places. They emerged toward the Great Red Shark. Shana blew her instrument, the Marsupial Flute, to call for help. And Manda played her instrument, a blue harp. Just as Tiblo and Martino heard the tune, they ran to the Great Red Shark. Just as they made it toward the ship, the bright green-colored lizard named, Scud, lit his light saber; two bars of green light appeared at both ends. He snarled at the heroes. The peg-legged minor monáchi named, Swatflea, lit his laser-curved nunchucks and swung them and swished them in front of himself. Tiblo and Martino readied their firearms.

"Come on," said Scud, "we've been through this before, Tigro."

"Well, you're not gonna get it," said Tiblo.

Scud swished his light saber. Tiblo fired his blasters, one shot damaged Scud's light saber. Swatflea threw his nunchucks. Tiblo dodged them. Suddenly, a major monáchi pirate knight shouted, "Report to the emperor!" Then all the pirate knights fled the area.

"And so," said Artidector. "I will grant you your individual ships." He showed the freedom fighters each of their own individual fighter ships behind him. As they entered the right colored ships, Zinger and the Invisi-Bot entered the Great Red Shark to start it up. And so, the team was just about ready to escape the Death Scale on their behalf.

Suddenly, four more henchmonsters appeared to attack: Tri-Psy-PO, Plag, Ice Brain, and Stargoyle. The freedom fighters started their ships as Zinger flew the Great Red Shark to the sky. The henchmonsters readied their abilities. Tiblo flew his red-orange ship with black stripes, the Tiger Shark, and shot amounts of twin lasers at Ice Brain. Ice Brain's robot body began to shed electricity. He shot his ice to freeze Martino's green bird-like ship, the Clover Bird. Ice Brain fell to the ground. He could use maintenance. Stargoyle began to blow a tornado. Plag spread his plague throughout the plain. Martino barrel-rolled with his ship out of the ice. Stargoyle's tornado emerged throughout midair. The freedom fighters could not resist. Tri-Psy-PO flashed his eye in the sky showing a swirl of hypnosis. Skinamar in his orange, round ship, the Ape Smacker, zoomed his boosting engine out of the behemoth. He shot his ship's plasma beams at Stargoyle and Tri-Psy-PO. Then he launched and threw a bomb among the monsters.

"Mm mm hwa ha ha," Plag laughed. "That tickles." His bones rose and fell to the ground. His skull rolled down a hill. "Oh, crap," he muttered.

Tri-Psy-PO's electric matter began to rage all around his framework. Stargoyle began to burst. He fell to the Death Scale's surface. The battle was won.

And so, the escape was made. The freedom fighters flew up to where Zinger and the Invisi-Bot flew the Great Red Shark. The freedom fighters flew their ships in the basement deck of which Artidector built for the ship.

Meanwhile, the Serpential pirate knights reported to the emperor as commanded.

"Find them in space," said the emperor. "Do not let them escape any further."

"As you wish," said Scud, saluting.

"They will wait to see my flying technique," said Darth Waternoose. The pirate knights left the throne room. They contacted other pirate knights to fly after the freedom fighters.

As the freedom fighters left the Death Scale's atmosphere, the Invisi-Bot heard an alert on the monitor.

"Enemy ships have arrived!" he shouted.

Tiblo and Martino ran to two ladders by the side walls of the ship. They went to one on the left. Tiblo climbed up to the top left machine gun while Martino climbed down to the bottom left. Beside them were tunnels that led to the machine gun cockpits on the other side. A small group of H-shaped ships surrounded the ship. Tiblo and Martino readied the machine guns, aiming for the enemy ships. They fired and fired. Tiblo shot one down.

"Ha ha heh heh! Gotcha!" he laughed.

Martino fired and fired until he shot another ship. "Got him," he said. "I got him!" he shouted to Tiblo above him.

"Great one, Marty!" Tiblo called back. "Don't get cocky!"

"There are three more out there, guys!" called Skinamar.

Tiblo and Martino concentrated on their fire. Tiblo shot another ship.

"YES!" he shouted, flinging his arm in front of himself.

Martino fired and fired until he shot the last two ships down simultaneously.

"We're all clear," he said.

"I thought we were goners," said Shana.

A message from Artidector flew through the freedom fighters' heads, "Just remember what your spirits already know, you have the force to conquer evil."

CHAPTER 20

THE HEAVENLY FEDERAL BASE

Just as the freedom fighters escaped the Death Scale's orbit, the Serpentials had made quite a mistake. The bodies from the shot down ships swam through space back to the Death Scale. The emperor hissed when he heard the mistake. The Serpential lieutenant, Fmee, who is a short hooked-beaked bird of prey, contacted the emperor.

"Our forces couldn't get hold of our enemies," he said.

"We'll have to try again," said the emperor. "They shall have to sacrifice their will of defeat among us. We must follow them."

"Yes, your majesty," said Fmee. He turned off the communication and his hologram vanished.

Meanwhile, the freedom fighters entered the Orion Nebula. They flew into a horse head. Inside was a secret world. The Heavenly Federal base was hidden there. As they entered it, a large forest appeared. Just ahead, there was a tarmac part of a spaceport. Tiblo landed the Great Red Shark. The freedom fighters walked to the base's giant central building.

As they reunited with the federation, the Death Scale moved closer to the horse head of the nebula.

"Entering the Orion Nebula," said the monitor, "the Heavenly Federal Base is hidden within the horse head at the far left."

Meanwhile, the freedom fighters went in the mission room, where the Heavenly Federal general, Gando Grizzle, a grizzly bear, told the pilots what he learned about the Sharp Empire's plans. As the freedom fighters took seats in the slope aisle, the general started his method turning on the giant computer screen, which showed a diagram of the Death Scale.

"Now that we've faced the enemy by final touch," said the general, "thanks to Captain Tigro finding more allies to protect our forces, me must fly toward the Death Scale . . ." the computer diagram zoomed in and moved up to show the north pole as the general pointed the narrow plastic rod. ". . . we have twenty minutes to live. One ship must fly up to the north pole or down to the south pole, using electron torpedoes to shoot down into one of the poles' holes flying straight down into the prime the tunnels of the prime meridian . . ." the diagram moved down with the image of the ship and torpedo, moving down to the part with the core. ". . . it should fly right at the core, which should destroy the biosphere." The diagram flashed.

"But that's impossible, even for a computer," said a male feline pilot sitting on the left of the freedom fighters.

"It's not impossible," Martino told him from a few chairs away. "We just have to give it all we've got."

"Yeah," said Skinamar, "he's right of course."

"Now," the general continued, "let's forgive our new freedom fighters that they were unable to save our federation's princess . . ."

"Not to worry, General," said Tiblo out loud. "It's all taken care of. Our holy friend, Artidector, knows how to manipulate the dead."

"Well," said the general, "that sums it." He stared at his watch, and then looked back at the audience saying, "Good luck, pilots, and ready your ships." All the pilots left the room along with the freedom fighters. The general left through the side door.

The Heavenly Federal pilots and the freedom fighters went into a huge hangar with many ships of the same color held in long rows. The Great Red Shark was double-parked at the far end by the metal gate.

"Hey, Calico!" Tiblo called to a male feline pilot. "Watch over my human partner in flight!"

"Will do," said the pilot.

As robots were packing the electron torpedoes in each ship's firing system, all pilots rolled kiosks toward one side of each ship. The pilots climbed into their seats, wearing helmets with eye shields.

And so, the pilots began to take off as the metal gate opened. The pilots zoomed out the gate as Tiblo began to fly the Great Red Shark behind them all.

Meanwhile, in the map room by the cargo bay, General Grizzle turned on a two-dimensional map on a cylinder table. The other Heavenly Federal officers sat on plastic chairs or stood by the general. The map displayed the horse head and the Death Scale.

"Death Scale approaching in 17 minutes," said the monitor. And the war is on.

CHAPTER 21

THE WAR

The Heavenly Federal pilots stood guard in their ships. The Death Scale was just about a mile ahead.

"All pilots stand by," the general said through the communication system connected to all the ships.

"Gold 1 standing by," said a male canine pilot.

"Silver 3 standing by," said a male feline pilot.

"Gold 4 standing by," said a female canine pilot.

"Bronze 2 standing by," said another male feline pilot.

"Silver 5 standing by," said a female feline pilot.

"Bronze leader standing by," said another male canine pilot. All pilots assigned so on and so forth.

The Death Scale was slowly moving toward the horse head as the pilots approached it.

"Look at the size of that thing," said the male feline pilot named, Calico.

All of the pilots zoomed into war. As they did, the Serpential pirate knights climbed into their ships and zoomed out of the docking bays at each outer end of Serpentopolis.

"Looks like we've got company," said a male canine pilot.

The henchmonsters also showed up to protect the biosphere. Sparxcalibur spread his lightning to electrocute some of the pilots. Two pilots were shot down. The freedom fighters flew down toward the surface.

"I'll cover us," said Shana. She flew her blue, long-footed ship, the Wallaby Wing in a loop. She shot arc lasers toward the pirate knight ships following the others. A male canine pilot hovered and flew up the northern hemisphere with his targeting computer on.

Meanwhile, Darth Waternoose and the twin viceroys left the emperor's throne room and went to the north docking bay.

In the Heavenly Federal base's map room, the monitor said, "Death Scale approaching in 10 minutes."

In Serpentopolis's targeting room, the Kassows looked at the computer of the map of how far away the horse head was.

"Our enemies will soon know not to have manipulated us," said Captain Kerbano Kassow, who is Governor Kassow's brother.

Meanwhile, Stargoyle appeared to create thunderstorms and tornadoes over the Death Scale.

"This is Gold 1," said that one canine pilot. "I'm going in." He flew towards the north pole. Just as his targeting computer marked the lock on the pole, he launched his electron torpedoes, but they went straight instead of in the hole. "Negative, negative, it didn't go in," said the pilot.

Suddenly, he noticed two ships above him. "Whoa, s***!" he said panicking. He tried to fly away, but a ship shot him down with a twin zapper. "This is Gold 1. I'm done for!" he said through the communicator. His ship fell to the Death Scale's surface and exploded.

The zapper came from Darth Waternoose's round, brown ship, the Flying Crab. He flew with the twin vulture viceroys' ship, the Duo of Volts, which had two pilot cockpits, both with firearms.

"Secure every section of the biosphere," said Waternoose.

"Roger, my lord," said Hooker and Blunt, as they made their flight while Waternoose flew down to the southern hemisphere.

Meanwhile, the Kassows watched the computer diagram of the horse head, as the Death Scale was moving closer.

"Death Scale approaching in 5 minutes," said the Heavenly Federal base's monitor.

Flying droids emerged through the Death Scale's skies. Regulto, in his yellow three-horned ship, the Golden Triceros, would manage to shoot many enemies around him, but he was just afraid to try.

"Just do your thing," said the voice of Rufus the Beast in his head. "I trust you can do one of the best." Regulto launched a bomb that blew all the flying droids surrounding him.

Worm droids emerged toward a group of pilots. Manda, in her purple wolf-headed ship, the Marine Wolf, shot twin lasers toward the heads and tails. The droids exploded part by part toward the pilots as they fled.

A female canine pilot flew down the southern hemisphere. "This is Silver 6, I'm going in," she said. She turned on her targeting computer, flying through a trench within the south polar cap of dry ice. Darth Waternoose and the Volton brothers approached among the cap toward the pilot.

"Stay on target," said one of the pilot leaders.

"I'm concentrating," said the Silver 6 pilot. Waternoose locked his target on the pilot, and then he fired his zapper, which shot her down.

According to the monitor, the Heaven Federation had only two minutes to live. The Kassows watched the shortening distance of the horse head. Would this be an Armageddon for the Heaven Federation or *can* a pilot destroy the biosphere in one piece?

And so, Tiblo and Martino flew toward the north pole.

"This is the Clover Bird, I'm going in," said Martino as he flew down and zoomed toward the pole.

Tiblo spotted sudden enemies boosting up the northern hemisphere on his monitor screen. He performed a long, wide loop for the enemies to not find him. So he decided if those enemies came toward Martino, he can protect him from being shot down. The enemies passing by were Waternoose and the Volton brothers.

Martino zoomed toward the pole over the grassy polar cap, with his targeting computer on. Suddenly, Artidector's voice came through his head, "Use the force, Martino." Waternoose and the Volton brothers zoomed among the north polar cap.

"Let go," Artidector's voice continued. Martino waited for the target lock. "Martino, trust me," Artidector's voice said. Obediently, Martino turned off his targeting computer.

"Clover Bird's target has been canceled," said the Heavenly Federal base monitor.

"Marty, you switched off your targeting computer," said General Grizzle, "what's wrong?"

"Nothing," said Martino, "I'm alright. I got a better idea." He carefully flew toward the pole. Waternoose and the Volton brothers hovered behind him.

"Lord Waternoose," said Hooker, "it's one of our enemies' freedom fighters."

"Let me handle him," said Waternoose.

"As you wish," said both of the Volton brothers. Waternoose flew between their halves of their ship as it split open.

Meanwhile, the Death Scale's approach finally confronted the horse head.

"The Heavenly Federal base is in range," said Commander Kassow.

"You may fire when ready," said his father.

Waternoose's target locked on the Clover Bird. "I have you now," he said. He was about to fire his double zapper, but Tiblo shot his lasers at his ship and the Volton brothers' ship. The two ships bounced against the sides of the trench. Then they flung out of it. Waternoose and the Volton brothers spun away from the Death Scale.

"You're all clear, Marty!" said Tiblo. "Now, let's blow this thing and go home!"

"Right!" said Martino. He shot his electron torpedoes. The force in his imagination pushed them into the hole in front of the north pole. "Okay!" he said. "Let's go!" He and Tiblo flew back to the horse head.

So, the Serpential officers started to activate the Death Scale's firing system. The Kassows watched with their covert feathers under the bases of their beaks. Suddenly, an explosion in the core blasted through the equator and the prime meridian. The Death Scale blew up into four major pieces along with the tiny particles within. A laser beam shot out of the eye of Serpentopolis that shot far, far away and out of the Orion Nebula.

"Great shot, Marty, that was one in a million!" Tiblo said. He and Martino flew back into the horse head.

CHAPTER 22

THEY'RE DONE

As Tiblo and Martino, along with the other freedom fighters and the rest of the Heavenly Federal pilots flew back to the base, Artidector's voice said, "Remember, the force will be with you. Always."

All pilots and freedom fighters entered the base's hangar, landing their ships where they were in the first place. The Heavenly Federal officers entered the place.

"Well done, pilots," said General Grizzle. "I would be honored to have the freedom fighters part of our forces."

"We lost five pilots," said Tiblo.

"Hey, Captain!" called the feline pilot named, Calico. "Wonderful timing." He saluted and flung his paw away from his forehead.

Zinger and the Invisi-Bot went out of the Great Red Shark.

"All thanks to human friend, Martin Izodorf," said Tiblo, getting Martino's name wrong, "he was brave enough to use the force, all because of . . ." A sudden thump on the roof of the hangar occurred. A hatch on the ceiling opened. It was Artidector. He lowered himself on the hangar's floor. The pilots were surprised of this giant white bird.

"These freedom fighters have the greatest intelligence in my philosophy," he said. "I had sent my two apprentices, Manda and Shana to your captain. I have also discovered that this young human being as for first of his species within a dream of animals. My children await me now. Good luck." He flew back up to the ceiling hatch. The hatch closed.

"Another one of these happy things," said the general, scratching the back of his head, "we'll press into reality." He and the other officers left the hangar through the door.

And so, the pilots left the hangar. The freedom fighters followed Zinger into another room. He led them into a small lounge with a wide, round plastic table and solid plastic chairs. The freedom fighters sat down as Zinger began his method.

"My previous apprentice, Nala Boomer, could never stand a chance," he said. "She once fought the emperor's henchmonsters and made it through in one piece. The only master who betrayed her was Dermazzo Joustiáño, a clever dragon who made moves, hovering over ground when he trained her. He was chosen as a count for the Sharp Empire.

"Much of this federation had always been attempted to protect its fortress, but they never stood a chance. Emperor Sharp had built and run many strange plans to find his enemies and demolish children's philosophies by canceling their favorite TV shows and destroying any world that only exists in fairy tales, using his biosphere's weapon of mass destruction. That's how Neverland had totally blown away."

"That all sounds strange," said Shana, rubbing her cheeks.

"That's just one of the greatest stories you've ever told me, Zinger," said Martino.

Zinger looked at an atomic clock that said 13:05. "Suppose that's our lunch break," he said. He hovered from perching on the top of a chair. The freedom fighters followed him out the door and into the hallway of solid tile floor. As they walked down the hallway, thoughts began to arise.

"So, Tiblo, what was it like to train such young females as a male?" asked Skinamar.

"Don't worry about it," said Tiblo. "It's not like they tell jokes or ridiculous stories."

"Hmmm . . . okay, that was a messed up question," said Skinamar. So the team went to the feast hall.

CHAPTER 23

ONE MISTAKE

On the northwestern quarter of the Death Scale, in the city of Serpentopolis, the Kassows had to report to the emperor about their first mistake.

"This is the time our first mistake existed," said Captain Kerbano Kassow.

"Don't worry," said the emperor. "The Heaven Federation cannot last. But we shall until they finally sacrifice their brute strength. Our immortality is like any heaven in space."

Meanwhile, Darth Waternoose and the two viceroys arrived back to the city in the north docking bay. They headed for the elevator to the throne room. Waternoose was to report to the emperor. Then he and the Volton brothers rode the central elevator up to the throne room. As they got there, Waternoose explained, "Our enemies are beginning to take control of the universal force."

"Perhaps just to cheat on us," said Blunt.

"They can't get that kind of point," said Hooker.

"We shall crush them using our personal alliances," said the emperor.

"They will abuse the force—or die," said Waternoose.

CHAPTER 24

THE CEREMONY

After the Heaven Federation's lunch break, a ceremony was run. Artidector had made medals for those who were able to destroy the Death Scale in time. Tiblo and Martino walked through the seat aisle up to the stage. No one talked throughout the ceremony. Artidector watched over the freedom fighters as the others remained seated, while Tiblo and Martino walked upon the stage. The general took the medals from the wall with hooks. He gave Martino the gold medal with the purple ribbon for he was the very one to destroy the Death Scale. He gave Tiblo the silver medal with the orange ribbon for he acted as a good defender to the federation. Tiblo and Martino faced the audience. As they did, a message from Artidector flowed through their heads, saying, "The galaxy will always last, because of you. And for the Sharp Empire's weakened plans, they will still be your nemeses."

THE WAR IS NOT OVER

Because of what Artidector said to the freedom fighters, they shall still be able to overcome the schemes of the Sharp Empire. All soldiers and pilots may have the right to believe in the extraordinary stories of space. The Serpentials should have made several attempts to manipulate the philosophy of dreams throughout youthful minds, and so on and so forth.